Anna Grossnickle Hines

WHAT JOE SAW

Greenwillow Books, New York

Joe was the last one to line up
for the walk to the park.

So nobody saw what Joe saw.

"Hurry up, Joe.
You have to keep up,"
Mrs. Murphy said.

But she didn't see what Joe saw.

"Come on, Pokey Joe,"
said Pete, who was first in line.
"You'll make us take all day."

But he didn't see what Joe saw.

"He's just a slowpoke," said Janet.
"Slowpoke, Pokey Joe," sang Dustin.
Janet, Pete, and Tisha joined in the chant.
"Slowpoke, Pokey Joe. Slowpoke, Pokey Joe."
"That's enough," said Mrs. Murphy. "Come on, Joe.
Hurry up now. We want to see the ducks, don't we?"

But none of them saw what Joe saw.

At the pond everyone crowded around
looking for the ducks.
"There they are!" screeched Pete.
"Where? Where?"
"Oh, there they are! There they are!"
everyone shouted.

Joe saw what everyone saw.

Mrs. Murphy got out the cracked corn,
and each child took a handful.
"Here, ducks. Here, ducks. Come and get it.
Come and get some corn," they called.

Soon Mrs. Murphy called, "Time to go."
The children scrambled to get in line.
Pete was first again, and Joe was last.

So nobody saw what Joe saw.

"Pete, you need to stop and tie your shoelace,"
said Mrs. Murphy.

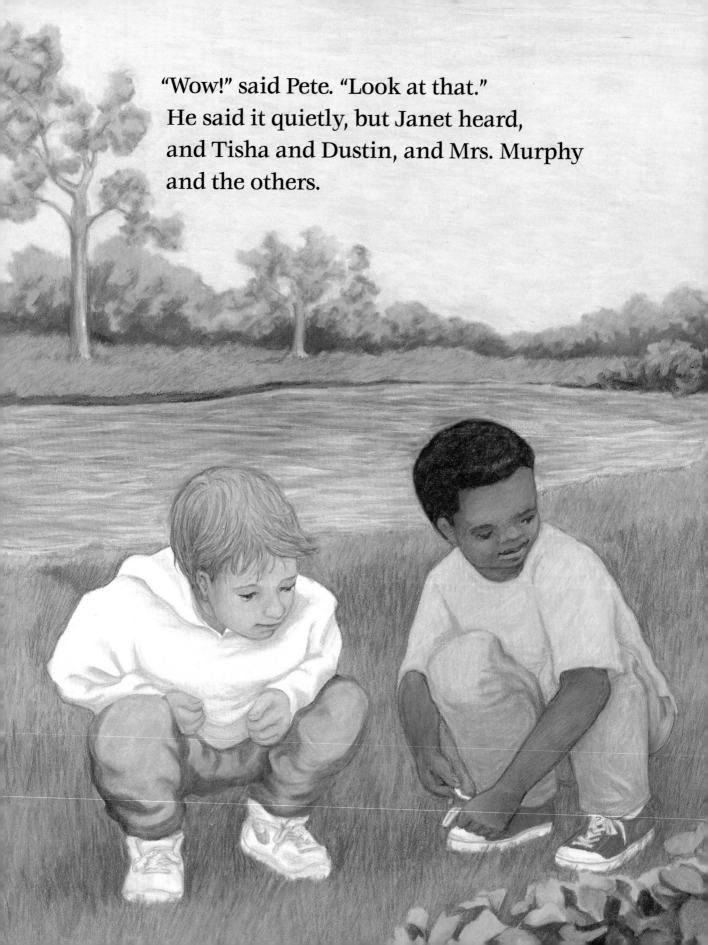

"Wow!" said Pete. "Look at that."
He said it quietly, but Janet heard,
and Tisha and Dustin, and Mrs. Murphy
and the others.

Then everyone saw what Joe saw.

TO SARAH AND NATHAN,
WHO TAKE TIME TO SEE

WATERCOLOR PAINTS AND COLORED PENCILS
WERE USED FOR THE FULL-COLOR ART.
THE TEXT TYPE IS VELJOVIC BOOK.

PRINTED IN HONG KONG BY SOUTH CHINA
PRINTING COMPANY (1988) LTD.

FIRST EDITION   10 9 8 7 6 5 4 3 2 1

LIBRARY OF CONGRESS
CATALOGING-IN-PUBLICATION DATA

HINES, ANNA GROSSNICKLE
WHAT JOE SAW / BY ANNA GROSSNICKLE HINES.
P.   CM.
SUMMARY: JOE IS THE LAST ONE IN HIS CLASS
TO LINE UP FOR A WALK TO THE PARK, AND HE
LAGS BEHIND ALL THE OTHERS, BUT HE SEES
A LOT MORE THAN THEY DO.
ISBN 0-688-13123-9 (TRADE).
ISBN 0-688-13124-7 (LIB. BDG.)
[1. NATURE—FICTION.]   I. TITLE.
PZ7.H572WH   1994   [E]—dc20   93-26583
CIP   AC